Willie the WHINER

by Mavis Smith

WHISTLESTOP ®

Troll Associates

For Matt the brat

"Time to get up," called Willie's mother. "Breakfast in five minutes!"

"Coming!" said Willie's little sister, Jessie.

"Be right there, Mom," yelled Willie's older brother, Kyle.

"Oh, Mom," groaned Willie, "do I have to get up? I'm tired. I want to sleep."

"Yes, Willie," his mother replied. "If you're tired, we'll have to make sure you get to bed extra early tonight."

"But I hate going to bed early," Willie whined. He crawled out of bed and stomped into the kitchen.

Willie's mother brought a big stack of pancakes to the table.

"Yippee!" said Jessie.

"Yummy!" said Kyle.

"What a nice treat!" said Willie's father.

"Don't we have any waffles, Mom?" whined Willie.

Willie's mom gave him a look. "No, we don't have any waffles, Willie," she said. "And even if we did, I'm certainly not going to make them for a boy who whines all day."

"I'm not whining," Willie whined.

After breakfast, Willie got dressed. "Where are my orange socks?" he called.

"They're in the wash," said his father. "Why don't you wear the green ones instead?"

"I don't want to wear the green ones," moaned Willie. "They're really itchy."

"Did you remember to brush your teeth?" asked Willie's father.

"Aw, Dad," cried Willie, "I just brushed them last night. And how come we never get the good toothpaste with the pink stripes?"

Willie's father rolled his eyes. "I'm getting a little tired of all your whining," he said. "Now finish dressing and brush your teeth."

After he brushed his teeth, Willie got out his trucks.

"You'll have to move, dear," said his mother. "You're in the way here."

"Why?" wailed Willie. "I like this room. I was here first."

Willie's mother sighed. "I'm sorry, honey, but right now I need to get some work done," she said. "You can play in the backyard."

"Yuck," grumbled Willie as he reluctantly moved his things. "There are worms in the backyard."

Willie stomped outside with his trucks.
"Hey, Willie," said Kyle, "let's play catch."
"I want to play, too!" said Jessie.
"No way," cried Willie. "She can't play. She's just a baby!"
"We can throw it to her for a little while," said Kyle. He tossed the ball gently to Jessie.

Willie stood with his hands on his hips. "This is so boring!" he whined.

Then Kyle threw the ball to Willie. Willie missed it.
"No fair!" he shouted as he tossed the ball back to Kyle. "I wasn't ready!"
Kyle rolled his eyes. He started to throw the ball again.

"Wait!" yelled Willie.

"Now what?" said Kyle, exasperated.

"My socks feel funny," said Willie. "They're all twisted. And my shoelaces are too tight, and my arm—"

"Willie," Kyle interrupted, "stop whining and just play!"

"I'm not whining," Willie whined.

Willie played by himself the rest of the day. After dinner he headed back outside.

"Put on a jacket, Willie," called his mother. "It's getting cold out."

"But I don't need a jacket," Willie moaned. "You never make Kyle wear a jacket."

"Honestly, Willie!" said his mother. "Just once I wish you'd do something without whining!"

"I don't whine," mumbled Willie to himself. He went outside and started to play.

After a while he heard his mother calling.
"Willie, it's time to come in," she said. "There's a treat—"
"But Mom," Willie interrupted, "I just started playing. It's not bedtime yet. I don't feel like coming inside. Why do I always have to come in so early? And how come—"

"That's enough, Willie!" his mother said. "The whole family is tired of your constant whining. If you want to stay out here, suit yourself!" Then she turned and went back into the house. Willie picked up his shovel and started digging again.

"Maybe I *will* stay out here all night," he said to himself. Willie was so busy playing that he didn't notice the dark clouds overhead. Suddenly a big raindrop plopped on his head.

Then it started to pour.

"Oh, no!" wailed Willie as he grabbed his toys and started running for the house.

THUNK! He tripped on a rock and slid across a big squishy mud puddle.

Then he went tumbling through the hedge.

"Aaaaaaaaagh!" cried Willie as he scrambled up the porch and reached for the back door.

Then he stopped.

Everyone was sitting around the kitchen table, talking and laughing—Mom, Dad, Kyle, and Jessie. And there in the center of the table was an empty ice cream container.

Willie gulped. "Is that Banana Crunch Delight ice cream?" Banana Crunch Delight was Willie's favorite flavor.

"It used to be," said Willie's father.

"We ate it all up," said Jessie.

"Now upstairs, everybody—it's time for bed," said Willie's mother.

"Good night, Mom. Good night, Dad," said Jessie.

"Thanks for the great dessert," said Kyle. "'Night."

Willie looked at the empty bowls in the sink.
He looked at his dad.
He looked at his mom.
He looked at the dab of Banana Crunch Delight on his sister's chin.
Then Willie opened his mouth...

...and decided not to whine!

"Good night," he said with a sheepish grin. "I'll see you in the morning."